The Twelve Days of Christmas

Illustrated by Cathie Shuttleworth

CLIVEDEN PRESS

On the first day of Christmas,
My true love sent to me
A partridge in a pear tree.

On the second day of Christmas,
My true love sent to me
Two turtle doves, and
A partridge in a pear tree.

On the third day of Christmas,
My true love sent to me
Three French hens,
Two turtle doves, and
A partridge in a pear tree.

On the fourth day of Christmas,
My true love sent to me
Four calling birds,
Three French hens,
Two turtle doves, and
A partridge in a pear tree.

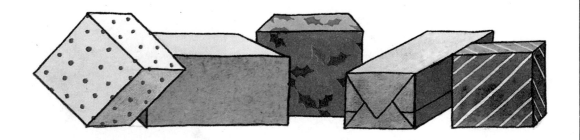

On the fifth day of Christmas,
My true love sent to me
Five gold rings,
Four calling birds,
Three French hens,
Two turtle doves, and
A partridge in a pear tree.

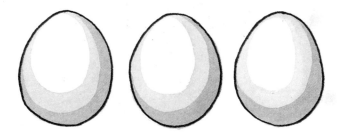

On the sixth day of Christmas,
My true love sent to me
Six geese a-laying,
Five gold rings,
Four calling birds,
Three French hens,
Two turtle doves, and
A partridge in a pear tree.

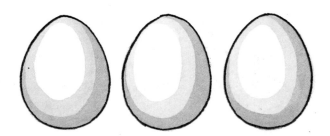

On the seventh day of Christmas,
My true love sent to me
Seven swans a-swimming,
Six geese a-laying,
Five gold rings,
Four calling birds,
Three French hens,
Two turtle doves, and
A partridge in a pear tree.

On the eighth day of Christmas,
My true love sent to me
Eight maids a-milking,
Seven swans a-swimming,
Six geese a-laying,
Five gold rings,
Four calling birds,
Three French hens,
Two turtle doves, and
A partridge in a pear tree.

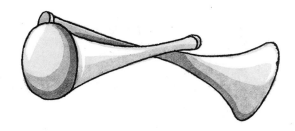

On the ninth day of Christmas,
My true love sent to me
Nine pipers piping,
Eight maids a-milking,
Seven swans a-swimming,
Six geese a-laying,
Five gold rings,
Four calling birds,
Three French hens,
Two turtle doves, and
A partridge in a pear tree.

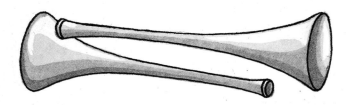

On the tenth day of Christmas,
My true love sent to me
Ten drummers drumming,
Nine pipers piping,
Eight maids a-milking,
Seven swans a-swimming,
Six geese a-laying,
Five gold rings,
Four calling birds,
Three French hens,
Two turtle doves, and
A partridge in a pear tree.

On the twelfth day of Christmas,
My true love sent to me
Twelve ladies dancing,
Eleven lords a-leaping,
Ten drummers drumming,
Nine pipers piping,
Eight maids a-milking,
Seven swans a-swimming,
Six geese a-laying,
Five gold rings,
Four calling birds,
Three French hens,
Two turtle doves, and
A partridge in a pear tree.